This book belongs to

_____

_____

_____

Goldilocks and the Three BARs

(BEYOND AVAILABLE RESOURCES)

Goldilocks and the Three BARs
(Beyond Available Resources)

Text copyright © 2014 by Ryan Forsythe
Illustrations copyright © 2014 by Rory Forsythe-Elder

Special thanks to Dan Mancuso and the *Illinois Valley News* for use
of the actual 'Rural Patrol' files for designing this book's final page

First Left Fork edition, December 2014
ISBN 1-978-0692330609

Any similarity between characters and
events depicted and actual people and events in
Josephine County is purely intentional.

Left Fork Books
O'Brien, Oregon

Goldilocks and the Three BARs

(BEYOND AVAILABLE RESOURCES)

written by
Ryan Forsythe

illustrated by
Rory Forsythe-Elder

Left Fork

ONCE UPON A TIME

there were Three Bears, who lived together in the woods of Josephine County, Oregon. One of the bears was a wee little Baby Bear, one was a medium-sized Mama Bear, and one was a great huge Papa Bear.

Each bear had a pot for their porridge—a wee little pot for Baby Bear, a medium-sized pot for Mama Bear, and a great huge pot for Papa Bear.

And they each had a chair to sit in—a wee little chair for Baby Bear, a medium-sized chair for Mama Bear, and a great huge chair for Papa Bear. And they each had a bed to sleep in—yes, you guessed it—a wee little bed for Baby Bear, a medium-sized bed for Mama Bear, and a great huge bed for Papa Bear.

One day, after they had made porridge for breakfast and poured it into their porridge pots, they went for a walk in the woods while the porridge cooled.

A few miles from the woods in which the home of the Three Bears stood, there lived an adventurous young lady. And from having bright golden curls, she called herself Goldilocks. She was roaming through the woods when she came upon the home of the Three Bears. She peeped in the window to make sure no one was home, and then opened the door and walked right in.

Kind of like she owned the place.

At the table in the kitchen, she found three pots of porridge. Now Goldilocks had the munchies and so she tasted the porridge from the first pot. "This porridge is too hot!" she exclaimed.

She tasted the porridge from the second pot. "This porridge is too cold!" she said. She tasted the last pot of porridge, and said "Ahhh, now this is just right." Then she ate it all up!

After eating the Three Bears' breakfast,
she was getting sleepy. In the living room, she
found three chairs. She sat in the first chair, but
soon exclaimed, "This chair is ginormous!"

She sat in the second chair and whined,
"This one is also much too big."

She tried the last and smallest chair. "Ahhh," she said. "Now this is just right."

But just as she settled down to rest, the chair broke apart. Clearly the Three Bears had not purchased their chairs from Kauffman Wood.

crack!

By this time Goldilocks was very tired, so she went upstairs in search of the bedroom.

She lay down in the first bed, but said, "This bed is too hard." She tried the second bed and said, "This one is too soft." Goldilocks tried the third bed. "Ahhh," she said. "Now this is what I'm talking about!"

And then she fell asleep.

As she was sleeping, the Three Bears
returned from their stroll in the woods.

In the kitchen, Papa Bear noticed his pot.
"Someone's been eating my porridge!"

Mama Bear saw her pot and said,
"Someone's been eating my porridge, too!"

"You're lucky," said Baby Bear. "Cuz
someone's been eating my porridge and they
ate it all up!"

Now Papa Bear, being concerned for his family, decided to seek assistance in the matter of the porridge robbery. He called the Josephine County Sheriff's office.

A recorded voice told him,

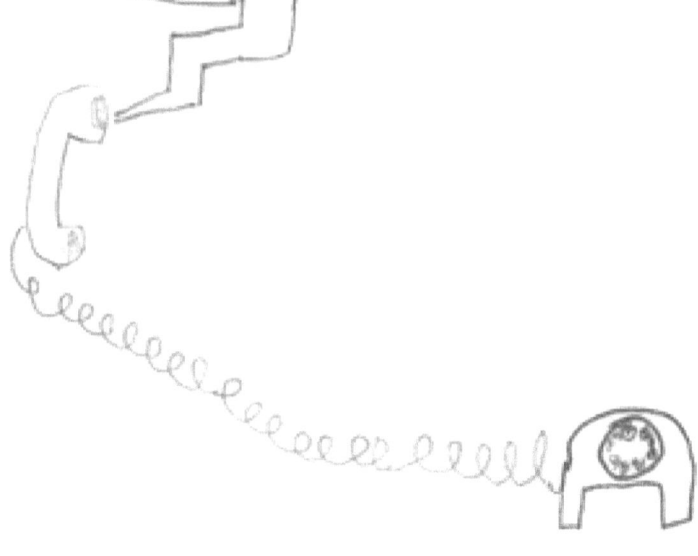

"Due to budgetary constraints, we are only able to answer the phone from 9 a.m. to 3:30 p.m. If you need assistance outside these hours, perhaps you should consider relocating to an area with adequate law enforcement services."

While Papa was on the phone, Mama Bear and Baby Bear had wandered to the living room. After cooling off some, Papa Bear joined them.

"Look—someone's been sitting in my chair," said Mama Bear.

Papa Bear glanced at his own chair.
"Someone's been sitting in my chair!" he said.
"Someone's been sitting in my chair and
they've broken it
all to pieces,"
cried Baby
Bear.

Papa checked the clock. 9:02. He decided to again try calling the Josephine County Sheriff's office.

Papa Bear carefully explained to the dispatcher about the vandalism to the chair and robbery of their porridge.

"Sorry," said the dispatcher. "It's presently beyond available resources."

"What?" asked Papa Bear.

"Deputies are only available Monday through Friday from 8 a.m. to 4 p.m. Today is Saturday."

Papa Bear growled, "This is ridiculous."

The dispatcher said, "Yeah, it's unfortunate you guys don't have law enforcement out there."

With no help on the way, the Three Bears decided to look around some more and see what else might be broken or missing.

When they got upstairs to the bedroom, Papa Bear saw his bed and growled, "Someone's been sleeping in my bed!"

Mama Bear noticed her bed and said, "Someone's been sleeping in my bed, too."

"Uh, guys?" said Baby Bear. "Someone's been sleeping in my bed...and she's still there!"

The Three Bears saw Goldilocks asleep in Baby Bear's bed. They all backed away slowly, so as to not wake her. Humans scared them, as they had seen first-hand what humans could do to deer, raccoons, bears, and many other animals. Not to mention their own kind.

Downstairs, Baby Bear asked, "What are we going to do?"

Papa Bear said, "I'm totally freaking out right now. There's a human *in the house!*"

"Calm down, honey bear," said Mama Bear. "I'm going to call 9-1-1."

On the phone, Mama Bear carefully explained about the human breaking-and-entering, devouring porridge, smashing chairs, making herself at home in their bedroom, and possibly wanting to do them harm. The dispatcher listened, then transferred her to the State Police and Mama Bear repeated the entire story.

The State Police dispatcher said, "Uh, I don't have anybody to send out there. You know, obviously if she's inside the residence and assaults you, can you ask her to go away?"

The dispatcher also suggested they consider hiding somewhere in the house.

Just then, Goldilocks woke up and made her way downstairs, where she saw the Three Bears by the phone. She screamed, "Help!" Then she ran down the hall, opened the door, and ran away into the woods. And she never returned to the home of the Three Bears.

But other humans did. And they stole more than porridge and broke more than chairs. That still wasn't enough to prompt the bears to vote for $200 more in property taxes each year to cover adequate law enforcement.

To this day, if you are out in the woods of Josephine County, Oregon, you may see a bear or two. Be advised to turn and head in the other direction. Because if they suspect you of wanting to harm them or take their stuff, well, let's just say it's hard to know what they might do to you. And if you call the Sheriff's office for help, chances are pretty good that your concerns might end up termed "Beyond Available Resources."

The End

About
the Story

The author was inspired to adapt the Goldilocks story after reading the police blotter each week in the *Illinois Valley News*, and learning how often calls for help are termed "Beyond Available Resources."

The situation in Josephine County made national headlines in May 2013, when a desperate Oregon woman was assaulted in her own home. She had called 911 but the dispatcher told her that due to budget cuts, he couldn't send help. At the time, there were only four sheriff deputies in Josephine County, none of whom was available on evenings or weekends.

Many of the quotes from dispatchers in Mama Bear's and Papa Bear's phone calls come from the transcripts of this 911 call (including the dispatcher encouraging the caller to simply ask the person to go away) or from quotes made by the county Sheriff in other places.

About
the Artist

Rory Forsythe-Elder, age 9, enjoys reading, playing Pokemon, and ice cream. He does not enjoy beets.

About
the Author

Ryan Forsythe, age 41, enjoys writing, playing with his kids, and travel. And ice cream.

Tales fron

(Editor's Note: Factual information for 'Tales' is provided by official law enforcement agencies. All persons listed are innocent until proven guilty in a court of law. Charges can be amended or dismissed.)

***

Saturday

*At 9:02 a.m. a caller (name not in log/NIL) indicated his family had returned to their home and found their breakfast eaten and furniture broken. The call was termed "beyond available resources" (BAR) by Josephine County Sheriff's Office (JCSO).

*There was a report of a vehicle being stolen from N. Old Stage Road.

*A caller was said to have found the culprit of the earlier breakfast robbery (hmm...a serial cereal eater?) in the house. JCSO called it BAR and transferred the caller to OSP.

*Some sort of incident on Arrowhead Drive in O'Brien was complained about. Details were blocked in the log.

*A woman refused to leave a porch "because Tina Turner was inside the home." It was ascertained that Tina Turner was not in the house and the woman was trespassed.

Outside the Valley

*Among 14 calls were several residential burglaries and a home break-in resulting in damage to a

www.ingramcontent.com/pod-product-compliance
Lightning Source LLC
Chambersburg PA
CBHW022001130726
47903CB00014B/2701